TO BEST FRIENDS:
MY FIRST BEST FRIEND, MY NEW BEST FRIEND,
AND MY DOG BEST FRIEND
- C.R.

TO MY SUPER-BOY ZACCY,
AND HIS AMAZING MOM - THE BEAUTIFUL BECS
- D.C.

PUBLISHED BY TRISM BOOKS, DEERFIELD, IL, USA

THE ELITE TEAM: CODY HEART OF THE MOUNTAIN

TEXT COPYRIGHT © 2019 BY CODY RUNNELS
ILLUSTRATIONS COPYRIGHT © 2019 BY DYLAN COBURN
ALL RIGHTS RESERVED. NO PART OF THIS BOOK MAY BE USED OR REPRODUCED IN ANY MANNER
WITHOUT THE WRITTEN PERMISSION OF THE PUBLISHER.

THE ELITE TEAM: HEART OF THE MOUNTAIN/WRITTEN BY CODY RUNNELS; ILLUSTRATED BY DYLAN COBURN

ISBN 978-0-9985291-7-2

1. DIVERSITY - JUVENILE LITERATURE 2. WRESTLING - JUVENILE LITERATURE 3. FRIENDSHIP - JUVENILE LITERATURE
4. FANTASY - JUVENILE LITERATURE I.TITLE.
THE ARTWORK WAS CREATED DIGITALLY
BOOK DESIGN BY ERICA WEISZ; EDITED BY SAM WEISZ
PRINTED IN MALAYSIA

10 9 8 7 6 5 4 3 2 1
WWW.TRISMBOOKS.COM

THE ELITE TEAM

CODY HEART OF THE MOUNTAIN

STORY BY
CODY

ILLUSTRATIONS BY
DYLAN COBURN

TRISM BOOKS
TURNING PAGES. GROWING MINDS.

CODY RACED DOWN CLAW MOUNTAIN.

HE DARTED *PAST* THE RIVER, *NEAR* THE CAVE, AND *TOWARD* THE TRAIL. HE COULD HEAR *HIS DAD* CALLING.

CODY WAS *EXCITED* TO SHARE HIS ANNUAL *FATHER-SON TRIP* WITH HIS OTHER FAMILY, *THE ELITE TEAM*.

"ACROSS THE STONY *RIVER*, THROUGH THE *CAVES*, AND ON TOP OF THE *MOUNTAIN*, SITS A *SINGLE CLAW* IN THE TRUNK OF THE *TALLEST TWISTING TREE*...

THIS CLAW BELONGS TO THE RIGHTFUL *CHAMPION OF CLAW MOUNTAIN*."

"SOME HIKERS SAY THE **CLAW** COMES FROM THE PAW OF THE **BLUE-EYED WOLF** WHO CAN **SEE THE FARTHEST**...

WHILE OTHERS SAY THE **CLAW** BELONGS TO THE **LONG-NOSED BEAR** WHO CAN **SMELL FOR MILES.**"

"*EVERYONE* KNOWS THESE TWO ANIMALS *HATE* EACH OTHER FOR THEIR *DIFFERENCES.*"

DUSTY FINISHED, "EACH ANIMAL BELIEVES *HE* HAS *THE CLAW* THAT *RULES THE MOUNTAIN.*"

AFTER THE CAMPFIRE, *THE ELITE TEAM* WENT TO BED KNOWING THEY DID *NOT* WANT TO RUN INTO ANY BEAR *OR* WOLF *CLAWS* ON THIS TRIP.

THE NEXT MORNING THE ELITE TEAM WOKE UP TO THEIR NORMAL ROUTINE. *THREE SPLASHES* OF WATER ON THEIR FACES, *FOUR STRETCHES* TO THEIR TOES AND *FIVE LARGE BOWLS* OF WILD BLUEBERRIES.

DUSTY'S LEGEND OF *CLAW MOUNTAIN* SAT IN THE BACK OF THEIR MINDS WITH EACH SPOONFUL OF BLUEBERRIES.

READY TO *SWIM* THE CLEAREST WATER, *COLLECT* THE SMOOTHEST ROCK, AND *CLIMB* THE HIGHEST TRAIL, THE ELITE TEAM SET OUT TO *EXPLORE.*

MARTY, KENNY, AND ADAM FISHED AT THE RIVER.

THEY CALLED FOR CODY, *"WE FOUND THE LONG-NOSED BEAR!"* *TOGETHER* THEY *FISHED* THE CLEAR WATERS.

IT WASN'T LONG BEFORE *THE YOUNG BUCKS* AND *BRANDI* COULD BE HEARD IN THE DISTANCE.

CODY SPRINTED OVER.

THE WOLF'S *BIG BLUE EYES* LOCKED WITH *CODY, BRANDI, AND THE YOUNG BUCKS* AS THEY *HOWLED* BACK AND FORTH.

THE ELITE TEAM MET UP ON THEIR WAY BACK TO THE CAMPSITE, WHEN *SUDDENLY* CODY LOOKED UP TO *ROCKS CRASHING* ABOVE.

MARTY, KENNY, ADAM, AND THE BEAR **SWIRLED** AND **SPUN**. THE YOUNG BUCKS AND BRANDI **TUMBLED SIDE BY SIDE** WITH THE WOLF.

CODY **TWISTED** THROUGH THE MOUNTAIN.

HE LANDED WITH A SLAM.

AS CODY **OPENED** HIS EYES, HE FELT **TRANSFORMED** BY THE **SPELL OF THE MOUNTAIN.**

LOST BUT **NOT ALONE**, CODY **SEARCHED** FOR THE ELITE TEAM.

MARTY, KENNY, AND **ADAM** WERE CROUCHED DOWN WITH THE **BEAR.** THEY TOO WERE UNDER THE **SPELL** OF THE MOUNTAIN.

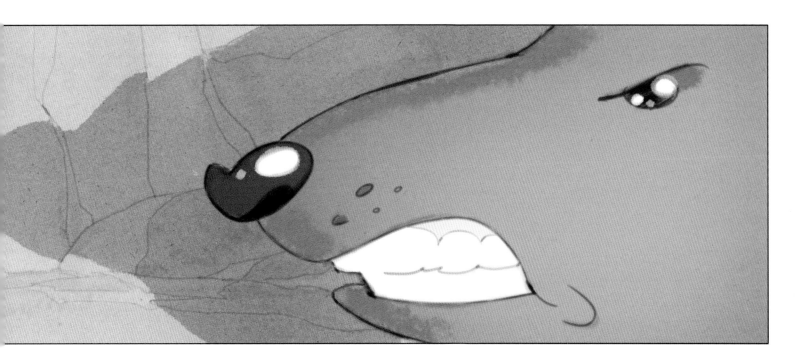

THE **WOLF** STOOD NEXT TO A **GROWING CREW.** IT WAS THE **YOUNG BUCKS** AND **BRANDI.** THEIR **BRIGHT BLUE EYES** STARED AT THE BEAR AND HIS TEAM.

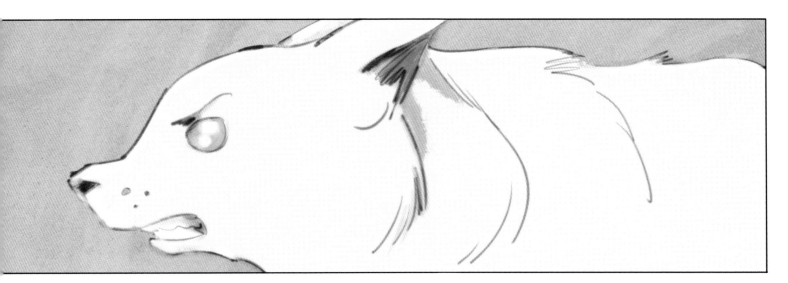

THEIR *EYES*...

THE *BEAR* WAS *JEALOUS* THAT HE COULD *NOT SEE* IN THE DARK.
THE *WOLF* WAS *JEALOUS* THAT HE COULD *NOT SMELL* HIS WAY BACK HOME.

MARTY, ADAM AND KENNY **CHANTED.**

MATT, NICK AND BRANDI **CHEERED.**

CODY HAD TO **FIND** A WAY TO BRING THE TEAM BACK **TOGETHER.**

CODY TURNED TO THE *BEAR*, *SCOOPED UP* HIS FURRY LEGS AND LANDED A *GIANT SWING*.

THE BEAR AND WOLF WERE MORE **POWERFUL UNITED.** THEY **WORKED AS ONE** TO LIGHT THE WAY AND SMELL FOR THE CAVE OPENING.

THE *HUGE PAW* OF *DUSTY* REACHED INTO THE LANDSLIDE, *GRABBED HOLD* OF *CODY*, WHO *HELD TIGHT* TO *BRANDI*, SO THAT THE REST OF *THE ELITE TEAM* COULD BE PULLED TO *SAFETY*.

CODY **CONNECTED** THE PAWS OF THE WOLF AND BEAR BEFORE SAYING GOODBYE.
THE ELITE TEAM **HONORED** THE **CHAMPIONS** OF CLAW MOUNTAIN.

THE TWO THAT FOUGHT FOR **GENERATIONS** OVER THEIR **DIFFERENCES** BEGAN THEIR RULE OVER CLAW MOUNTAIN **TOGETHER**.

HAPPY, EXHAUSTED, AND BACK SAFE, THE ELITE TEAM CELEBRATED, KNOWING THEY REWROTE THE LEGEND OF CLAW MOUNTAIN.